WAR AND PEACE
BOOK FOURTEEN : 1812

By Leo Tolstoy

Double 9
BOOKS

War and Peace Book 14
by Leo Tolstoy

ISBN: 978-93-94973-62-6

Published by

DOUBLE 9 BOOKS

2/13-B, Ansari Road
Daryaganj, New Delhi - 110002
info@double9books.com
www.double9books.com
Tel. 011-40042856

Printed in India.

About the Author

Leo Tolstoy was a Russian creator known for his books War and Peace which is viewed as the best book of pragmatist fiction. Tolstoy is additionally viewed as world's best author by quite a few people. Additionally an ethical scholar and a social reformer, Tolstoy had extreme moralistic points of view. In later life, he turned into an intense Christian rebel and anarcho-conservative.

Leo Tolstoy Born in Yasnaya Polyana on September 9, 1828, He had a place with a notable honorable Russian family. He was the fourth among five offspring of Count Nikolai Ilyich Tolstoy and Countess Mariya Tolstaya, both of whom kicked the bucket passing on their youngsters to be raised by family members.

In 1844, Tolstoy was acknowledged into Kazan University. Incapable to graduate past the subsequent year, Tolstoy got back to Yasnava Polyana and afterward invested energy going among Moscow and St. Petersburg. With some functioning information on a few dialects, he turned into a multilingual. Yet again the recently observed youth pulled in Tolstoy towards drinking, visiting massage parlors and most betting which left him in weighty obligation and anguish however Tolstoy before long acknowledged he was carrying on with a brutish life and endeavored college tests with the expectation that he would acquire a situation with the public authority, yet finished yet up in Caucuses serving in the military continuing in the strides of his senior sibling.

In Year 1862, Leo Tolstoy wedded Sophia Andreevna Behrs, generally called Sonya, who was 16 years more youthful than him. The couple had thirteen youngsters, of which, five passed on at an early age. Sonya went about as Tolstoy's secretary, editor and monetary chief while he made two out of his most prominent works. Their initial wedded life was loaded up with happiness.

He started composing his show-stopper, War and Peace in 1862. The six volumes of the work were distributed somewhere in the range of 1863 and 1869. With 580 characters got from history and others made by Tolstoy, this extraordinary novel takes on investigating the hypothesis of history and the irrelevance of noted figures like Alexander and Napoleon. Anna Karenina, Tolstoy's next epic was begun in 1873 and distributed totally in 1878.

Contents

BOOK FOURTEEN : 1812

CHAPTER I

The Battle of Borodinó, with the occupation of Moscow that followed it and the flight of the French without further conflicts, is one of the most instructive phenomena in history.

All historians agree that the external activity of states and nations in their conflicts with one another is expressed in wars, and that as a direct result of greater or less success in war the political strength of states and nations increases or decreases.

Strange as may be the historical account of how some king or emperor, having quarreled with another, collects an army, fights his enemy's army, gains a victory by killing three, five, or ten thousand men, and subjugates a kingdom and an entire nation of several millions, all the facts of history (as far as we know it) confirm the truth of the statement that the greater or lesser success of one army against another is the cause, or at least an essential indication, of an increase or decrease in the strength of the nation—even though it is unintelligible why the defeat of an army—a hundredth part of a nation—should oblige that whole nation to submit. An army gains a victory, and at once the rights of the conquering nation have increased to the detriment of the defeated. An army has suffered defeat, and at once a people loses its rights in proportion to the severity of the reverse, and if its army suffers a complete defeat the nation is quite subjugated.

So according to history it has been found from the most ancient times, and so it is to our own day. All Napoleon's wars serve to confirm this rule. In proportion to the defeat of the Austrian army Austria loses its rights, and the rights and the strength of France increase. The victories of the French at Jena and Auerstädt destroy the independent existence of Prussia.

But then, in 1812, the French gain a victory near Moscow. Moscow is taken and after that, with no further battles, it is not Russia that ceases to exist, but the French army of six hundred thousand, and then Napoleonic France itself. To strain the facts to fit the rules of history: to say that the field of battle at Borodinó remained in the hands of the Russians, or that after Moscow there were other battles that destroyed Napoleon's army, is impossible.

After the French victory at Borodinó there was no general engagement nor any that were at all serious, yet the French army ceased to exist. What does this mean? If it were an example taken from the history of China, we might say that it was not an historic phenomenon (which is the historians' usual expedient when anything does not fit their standards); if the matter concerned some brief conflict in which only a small number of troops took part, we might treat it as an exception; but this event occurred before our fathers' eyes, and for them it was a question of the life or death of their fatherland, and it happened in the greatest of all known wars.

The period of the campaign of 1812 from the battle of Borodinó to the expulsion of the French proved that the winning of a battle does not produce a conquest and is not even an invariable indication of conquest; it proved that the force which decides the fate of peoples lies not in the conquerors, nor even in armies and battles, but in something else.

The French historians, describing the condition of the French army before it left Moscow, affirm that all was in order in the Grand Army, except the cavalry, the artillery, and the transport—there was no forage for the horses or the cattle. That was a misfortune no one could remedy, for the peasants of the district burned their hay rather than let the French have it.

The victory gained did not bring the usual results because the peasants Karp and Vlas (who after the French had evacuated Moscow drove in their carts to pillage the town, and in general personally failed to manifest any heroic feelings), and the whole innumerable multitude of such peasants, did not bring their hay to Moscow for the high price offered them, but burned it instead.

Let us imagine two men who have come out to fight a duel with rapiers according to all the rules of the art of fencing. The fencing has gone on for some time; suddenly one of the combatants, feeling himself wounded and understanding that the matter is no joke but concerns his life, throws down his rapier, and seizing the first cudgel that comes to hand begins to brandish it. Then let us imagine that the combatant who so sensibly employed the best and simplest means to attain his end was at the same time influenced by traditions of chivalry and, desiring to conceal the facts of the case, insisted that he had gained his victory with the rapier according to all the rules of art. One can imagine what confusion and obscurity would result from such an account of the duel.

The fencer who demanded a contest according to the rules of fencing was the French army; his opponent who threw away the rapier and snatched up the cudgel was the Russian people; those who try to explain the matter according to the rules of fencing are the historians who have described the event.

After the burning of Smolénsk a war began which did not follow any previous traditions of war. The burning of towns and villages, the retreats after battles, the blow dealt at Borodinó and the renewed retreat, the burning of Moscow, the capture of marauders, the seizure of transports, and the guerrilla war were all departures from the rules.

Napoleon felt this, and from the time he took up the correct fencing attitude in Moscow and instead of his opponent's rapier saw a cudgel raised above his head, he did not cease to complain to Kutúzov and to the Emperor Alexander that the war was being carried on contrary to all the rules—as if there were any rules for killing people. In spite of the complaints of the French as to the nonobservance of the rules, in spite of the fact that to some highly placed Russians it seemed rather disgraceful to fight with a cudgel and they wanted to assume a pose *en quarte* or *en tierce* according to all the rules, and to make an adroit thrust *en prime*, and so on—the cudgel of the people's war was lifted with all its menacing and majestic strength, and without consulting anyone's tastes or rules and regardless of anything else, it rose and fell with stupid simplicity, but consistently, and belabored the French till the whole invasion had perished.

And it is well for a people who do not—as the French did in 1813—salute according to all the rules of art, and, presenting the hilt of their rapier gracefully and politely, hand it to their magnanimous conqueror, but at the moment of trial, without asking what rules others have adopted in similar cases, simply and easily pick up the first cudgel that comes to hand and strike with it till the feeling of resentment and revenge in their soul yields to a feeling of contempt and compassion.

CHAPTER II

O ne of the most obvious and advantageous departures from the so-called laws of war is the action of scattered groups against men pressed together in a mass. Such action always occurs in wars that take on a national character. In such actions, instead of two crowds opposing each other, the men disperse, attack singly, run away when attacked by stronger forces, but again attack when opportunity offers. This was done by the guerrillas in Spain, by the mountain tribes in the Caucasus, and by the Russians in 1812.

People have called this kind of war "guerrilla warfare" and assume that by so calling it they have explained its meaning. But such a war does not fit in under any rule and is directly opposed to a well-known rule of tactics which is accepted as infallible. That rule says that an attacker should concentrate his forces in order to be stronger than his opponent at the moment of conflict.

Guerrilla war (always successful, as history shows) directly infringes that rule.

This contradiction arises from the fact that military science assumes the strength of an army to be identical with its numbers. Military science says that the more troops the greater the strength. *Les grosbataillonsonttoujours raison.* *

* Large battalions are always victorious.

For military science to say this is like defining momentum in mechanics by reference to the mass only: stating that momenta are equal or unequal to each other simply because the masses involved are equal or unequal.

Momentum (quantity of motion) is the product of mass and velocity.

In military affairs the strength of an army is the product of its mass and some unknown x.

Military science, seeing in history innumerable instances of the fact that the size of any army does not coincide with its strength and that small detachments defeat larger ones, obscurely admits the existence of this unknown factor and tries to discover it—now in a geometric formation, now in the equipment employed, now, and most usually, in the genius of the commanders. But the assignment of these various meanings to the factor does not yield results which accord with the historic facts.

Yet it is only necessary to abandon the false view (adopted to gratify the "heroes") of the efficacy of the directions issued in wartime by commanders, in order to find this unknown quantity.

That unknown quantity is the spirit of the army, that is to say, the greater or lesser readiness to fight and face danger felt by all the men composing an army, quite independently of whether they are, or are not, fighting under the command of a genius, in two—or three-line formation, with cudgels or with rifles that repeat thirty times a minute. Men who want to fight will always put themselves in the most advantageous conditions for fighting.

The spirit of an army is the factor which multiplied by the mass gives the resulting force. To define and express the significance of this unknown factor—the spirit of an army—is a problem for science.

This problem is only solvable if we cease arbitrarily to substitute for the unknown x itself the conditions under which that force becomes apparent—such as the commands of the general, the equipment employed, and so on—mistaking these for the real significance of the factor, and if we recognize this unknown quantity in its entirety as being the greater or lesser desire to fight and to face danger. Only then, expressing known historic facts by equations and comparing the relative significance of this factor, can we hope to define the unknown.

Ten men, battalions, or divisions, fighting fifteen men, battalions, or divisions, conquer—that is, kill or take captive—all the others, while themselves losing four, so that on the one side four and on the other fifteen were lost. Consequently the four were equal to the fifteen, and therefore $4x = 15y$. Consequently $x/y = 15/4$. This equation does not give us the value of the unknown factor but gives us a ratio between two unknowns. And by bringing variously selected historic units (battles, campaigns, periods of war) into such equations, a series of numbers could be obtained in which certain laws should exist and might be discovered.

The tactical rule that an army should act in masses when attacking, and in smaller groups in retreat, unconsciously confirms the truth that the strength of an army depends on its spirit. To lead men forward under fire more discipline (obtainable only by movement in masses) is needed than is needed to resist attacks. But this rule which leaves out of account the spirit of the army continually proves incorrect and is in particularly striking contrast to the facts when some strong rise or fall in the spirit of the troops occurs, as in all national wars.

The French, retreating in 1812—though according to tactics they should have separated into detachments to defend themselves—congregated into a mass because the spirit of the army had so fallen that only the mass held the army together. The Russians, on the contrary, ought according to tactics to have attacked in mass, but in fact they split up into small units, because their spirit had so risen that separate individuals, without orders, dealt blows at the French without needing any compulsion to induce them to expose themselves to hardships and dangers.

CHAPTER III

The so-called partisan war began with the entry of the French into Smolénsk.

Before partisan warfare had been officially recognized by the government, thousands of enemy stragglers, marauders, and foragers had been destroyed by the Cossacks and the peasants, who killed them off as instinctively as dogs worry a stray mad dog to death. DenísDavýdov, with his Russian instinct, was the first to recognize the value of this terrible cudgel which regardless of the rules of military science destroyed the French, and to him belongs the credit for taking the first step toward regularizing this method of warfare.

On August 24 Davýdov's first partisan detachment was formed and then others were recognized. The further the campaign progressed the more numerous these detachments became.

The irregulars destroyed the great army piecemeal. They gathered the fallen leaves that dropped of themselves from that withered tree—the French army—and sometimes shook that tree itself. By October, when the French were fleeing toward Smolénsk, there were hundreds of such companies, of various sizes and characters. There were some that adopted all the army methods and had infantry, artillery, staffs, and the comforts of life. Others consisted solely of Cossack cavalry. There were also small scratch groups of foot and horse, and groups of peasants and landowners that remained unknown. A sacristan commanded one party which captured several hundred prisoners in the course of a month; and there was Vasílisa, the wife of a village elder, who slew hundreds of the French.

The partisan warfare flamed up most fiercely in the latter days of October. Its first period had passed: when the partisans themselves, amazed at their own boldness, feared every minute to be surrounded and captured by the French, and hid in the forests without unsaddling, hardly daring to dismount and always expecting to be pursued. By the end of October this kind of warfare had taken definite shape: it had become clear to all what could be ventured against the French and what could not. Now only the commanders of detachments with staffs, and moving according to rules at a distance from the French, still regarded many things as impossible. The small bands that had started their activities long before and had already observed the French closely considered things possible which the commanders of the big detachments did not dare to contemplate. The Cossacks and peasants who crept in among the French now considered everything possible.

On October 22, Denísov (who was one of the irregulars) was with his group at the height of the guerrilla enthusiasm. Since early morning he and his party had been on the move. All day long he had been watching from the forest that skirted the highroad a large French convoy of cavalry baggage and Russian prisoners separated from the rest of the army, which—as was learned from spies and prisoners— was moving under a strong escort to Smolénsk. Besides Denísov and Dólokhov (who also led a small party and moved in Denísov's vicinity), the commanders of some large divisions with staffs also knew of this convoy and, as Denísov expressed it, were sharpening their teeth for it. Two of the commanders of large parties—one a Pole and the other a German—sent invitations to Denísov almost simultaneously, requesting him to join up with their divisions to attack the convoy.

"No, bwother, I have gwownmustaches myself," said Denísov on reading these documents, and he wrote to the German that, despite his heartfelt desire to serve under so valiant and renowned a general, he had to forgo that pleasure because he was already under the command of the Polish general. To the Polish general he replied to the same effect, informing him that he was already under the command of the German.

Having arranged matters thus, Denísov and Dólokhov intended, without reporting matters to the higher command, to attack and seize that convoy with their own small forces. On October 22 it was moving from the village of Mikúlino to that of Shámshevo. To the left of the road between Mikúlino and Shámshevo there were large forests, extending in some places up to the road itself though in others a mile or more back from it. Through these forests Denísov and his party rode all day, sometimes keeping well back in them and sometimes coming to the very edge, but never losing sight of the moving French. That morning, Cossacks of Denísov's party had seized and carried off into the forest two wagons loaded with cavalry saddles, which had stuck in the mud not far from Mikúlino where the forest ran close to the road. Since then, and until evening, the party had watched the movements of the French without attacking. It was necessary to let the French reach Shámshevo quietly without alarming them and then, after joining Dólokhov who was to come that evening to a consultation at a watchman's hut in the forest less than a mile from Shámshevo, to surprise the French at dawn, falling like an avalanche on their heads from two sides, and rout and capture them all at one blow.

In their rear, more than a mile from Mikúlino where the forest came right up to the road, six Cossacks were posted to report if any fresh columns of French should show themselves.

Beyond Shámshevo, Dólokhov was to observe the road in the same way, to find out at what distance there were other French troops. They reckoned that the convoy had fifteen hundred men. Denísov had two hundred, and Dólokhov might have as many more, but the disparity of numbers did not deter Denísov. All that he now wanted to know was what troops these were and to learn that he had to capture a "tongue"—that is, a man from the enemy column. That morning's attack on the wagons had been made so hastily that the Frenchmen with the wagons had all been killed; only a little drummer boy had been taken alive, and as he was a straggler he could tell them nothing definite about the troops in that column.

Denísov considered it dangerous to make a second attack for fear of putting the whole column on the alert, so he sent TíkhonShcherbáty, a peasant of his party, to Shámshevo to try and seize at least one of the French quartermasters who had been sent on in advance.

CHAPTER IV

It was a warm rainy autumn day. The sky and the horizon were both the color of muddy water. At times a sort of mist descended, and then suddenly heavy slanting rain came down.

Denísov in a felt cloak and a sheepskin cap from which the rain ran down was riding a thin thoroughbred horse with sunken sides. Like his horse, which turned its head and laid its ears back, he shrank from the driving rain and gazed anxiously before him. His thin face with its short, thick black beard looked angry.

Beside Denísov rode an *esaul*, * Denísov's fellow worker, also in felt cloak and sheepskin cap, and riding a large sleek Don horse.

* A captain of Cossacks.

Esaul Lováyski the Third was a tall man as straight as an arrow, pale-faced, fair-haired, with narrow light eyes and with calm self-satisfaction in his face and bearing. Though it was impossible to say in what the peculiarity of the horse and rider lay, yet at first glance at the *esaul* and Denísov one saw that the latter was wet and uncomfortable and was a man mounted on a horse, while looking at the *esaul* one saw that he was as comfortable and as much at ease as always and that he was not a man who had mounted a horse, but a man who was one with his horse, a being consequently possessed of twofold strength.

A little ahead of them walked a peasant guide, wet to the skin and wearing a gray peasant coat and a white knitted cap.

A little behind, on a poor, small, lean Kirghíz mount with an enormous tail and mane and a bleeding mouth, rode a young officer in a blue French overcoat.

Beside him rode an hussar, with a boy in a tattered French uniform and blue cap behind him on the crupper of his horse. The boy held on to the hussar with cold, red hands, and raising his eyebrows gazed about him with surprise. This was the French drummer boy captured that morning.

Behind them along the narrow, sodden, cut up forest road came hussars in threes and fours, and then Cossacks: some in felt cloaks, some in French greatcoats, and some with horsecloths over their heads. The horses, being drenched by the rain, all looked black whether chestnut or bay. Their necks, with their wet, close-clinging manes, looked strangely thin. Steam rose from them. Clothes, saddles, reins, were all wet, slippery, and sodden, like the ground and the fallen leaves that strewed the road. The men sat huddled up trying not to stir, so as to warm the water that had trickled to their bodies and not admit the fresh cold water that was leaking in under their seats, their knees, and at the back of their necks. In the midst of the outspread line of Cossacks two wagons, drawn by French horses and by saddled Cossack horses that had been hitched on in front, rumbled over the tree stumps and branches and splashed through the water that lay in the ruts.

Denísov's horse swerved aside to avoid a pool in the track and bumped his rider's knee against a tree.

"Oh, the devil!" exclaimed Denísov angrily, and showing his teeth he struck his horse three times with his whip, splashing himself and his comrades with mud.

Denísov was out of sorts both because of the rain and also from hunger (none of them had eaten anything since morning), and yet more because he still had no news from Dólokhov and the man sent to capture a "tongue" had not returned.

"There'll hardly be another such chance to fall on a transport as today. It's too risky to attack them by oneself, and if we put it off till another day one of the big guerrilla detachments will snatch the prey from under our noses," thought Denísov, continually peering forward, hoping to see a messenger from Dólokhov.

On coming to a path in the forest along which he could see far to the right, Denísov stopped.

"There's someone coming," said he.

The *esaul* looked in the direction Denísov indicated.

"There are two, an officer and a Cossack. But it is not *presupposable* that it is the lieutenant colonel himself," said the *esaul*, who was fond of using words the Cossacks did not know.

The approaching riders having descended a decline were no longer visible, but they reappeared a few minutes later. In front, at a weary gallop and using his leather whip, rode an officer, disheveled and drenched, whose trousers had worked up to above his knees. Behind him, standing in the stirrups, trotted a Cossack. The officer, a very young lad with a broad rosy face and keen merry eyes, galloped up to Denísov and handed him a sodden envelope.

"From the general," said the officer. "Please excuse its not being quite dry."

Denísov, frowning, took the envelope and opened it.

"There, they kept telling us: 'It's dangerous, it's dangerous,'" said the officer, addressing the *esaul* while Denísov was reading the dispatch. "But Komaróv and I"—he pointed to the Cossack—"were prepared. We have each of us two pistols.... But what's this?" he asked, noticing the French drummer boy. "A prisoner? You've already been in action? May I speak to him?"

"Wostóv! Pétya!" exclaimed Denísov, having run through the dispatch. "Why didn't you say who you were?" and turning with a smile he held out his hand to the lad.

The officer was PétyaRostóv.

All the way Pétya had been preparing himself to behave with Denísov as befitted a grown-up man and an officer—without hinting at their previous acquaintance. But as soon as Denísov smiled at him Pétya brightened up, blushed with pleasure, forgot the official manner he had been rehearsing, and began telling him how he had already been in a battle near Vyázma and how a certain hussar had distinguished himself there.

"Well, I am glad to see you," Denísov interrupted him, and his face again assumed its anxious expression.

"Michael Feoklítych," said he to the *esaul*, "this is again fwom that German, you know. He"—he indicated Pétya—"is serving under him."

And Denísov told the *esaul* that the dispatch just delivered was a repetition of the German general's demand that he should join forces with him for an attack on the transport.

"If we don't take it tomowwow, he'll snatch it fwom under our noses," he added.

While Denísov was talking to the *esaul*, Pétya—abashed by Denísov's cold tone and supposing that it was due to the condition of his trousers—furtively tried to pull them down under his greatcoat so that no one should notice it, while maintaining as martial an air as possible.

"Will there be any orders, your honor?" he asked Denísov, holding his hand at the salute and resuming the game of adjutant and general for which he had prepared himself, "or shall I remain with your honor?"

"Orders?" Denísov repeated thoughtfully. "But can you stay till tomowwow?"

"Oh, please... May I stay with you?" cried Pétya.

"But, just what did the genewal tell you? To weturn at once?" asked Denísov.

Pétya blushed.

"He gave me no instructions. I think I could?" he returned, inquiringly.

"Well, all wight," said Denísov.

And turning to his men he directed a party to go on to the halting place arranged near the watchman's hut in the forest, and told the officer on the Kirghíz horse (who performed the duties of an adjutant) to go and find out where Dólokhov was and whether he would come that evening. Denísov himself intended going with the *esaul* and Pétya to the edge of the forest where it reached out to Shámshevo, to have a look at the part of the French bivouac they were to attack next day.

"Well, old fellow," said he to the peasant guide, "lead us to Shámshevo."

Denísov, Pétya, and the *esaul*, accompanied by some Cossacks and the hussar who had the prisoner, rode to the left across a ravine to the edge of the forest.

CHAPTER V

The rain had stopped, and only the mist was falling and drops from the trees. Denísov, the *esaul*, and Pétya rode silently, following the peasant in the knitted cap who, stepping lightly with outturned toes and moving noiselessly in his bast shoes over the roots and wet leaves, silently led them to the edge of the forest.

He ascended an incline, stopped, looked about him, and advanced to where the screen of trees was less dense. On reaching a large oak tree that had not yet shed its leaves, he stopped and beckoned mysteriously to them with his hand.

Denísov and Pétya rode up to him. From the spot where the peasant was standing they could see the French. Immediately beyond the forest, on a downward slope, lay a field of spring rye. To the right, beyond a steep ravine, was a small village and a landowner's house with a broken roof. In the village, in the house, in the garden, by the well, by the pond, over all the rising ground, and all along the road uphill from the bridge leading to the village, not more than five hundred yards away, crowds of men could be seen through the shimmering mist. Their un-Russian shouting at their horses which were straining uphill with the carts, and their calls to one another, could be clearly heard.

"Bwing the prisoner here," said Denísov in a low voice, not taking his eyes off the French.

A Cossack dismounted, lifted the boy down, and took him to Denísov. Pointing to the French troops, Denísov asked him what these and those of them were. The boy, thrusting his cold hands into his pockets and lifting his eyebrows, looked at Denísov in affright, but in spite of an evident desire to say all he knew gave confused answers, merely assenting to everything Denísov asked him. Denísov turned away from him frowning and addressed the *esaul*, conveying his own conjectures to him.

Pétya, rapidly turning his head, looked now at the drummer boy, now at Denísov, now at the *esaul*, and now at the French in the village and along the road, trying not to miss anything of importance.

"Whether Dólokhov comes or not, we must seize it, eh?" said Denísov with a merry sparkle in his eyes.

"It is a very suitable spot," said the *esaul*.

"We'll send the infantwy down by the swamps," Denísov continued. "They'll cweep up to the garden; you'll wide up fwom there with the Cossacks"—he pointed to a spot in the forest beyond the village—"and I with my hussars fwom here. And at the signal shot..."

"The hollow is impassable—there's a swamp there," said the *esaul*. "The horses would sink. We must ride round more to the left...."

While they were talking in undertones the crack of a shot sounded from the low ground by the pond, a puff of white smoke appeared, then another, and the sound of hundreds of seemingly merry French voices shouting together came up from the slope. For a moment Denísov and the *esaul* drew back. They were so near that they thought they were the cause of the firing and shouting. But the firing and shouting did not relate to them. Down below, a man wearing something red was running through the marsh. The French were evidently firing and shouting at him.

"Why, that's our Tíkhon," said the *esaul*.

"So it is! It is!"

"The wascal!" said Denísov.

"He'll get away!" said the *esaul*, screwing up his eyes.

The man whom they called Tíkhon, having run to the stream, plunged in so that the water splashed in the air, and, having disappeared for an instant, scrambled out on all fours, all black with the wet, and ran on. The French who had been pursuing him stopped.

"Smart, that!" said the *esaul*.

War and Peace

"What a beast!" said Denísov with his former look of vexation. "What has he been doing all this time?"

"Who is he?" asked Pétya.

"He's our *plastún*. I sent him to capture a 'tongue.'"

"Oh, yes," said Pétya, nodding at the first words Denísov uttered as if he understood it all, though he really did not understand anything of it.

TíkhonShcherbáty was one of the most indispensable men in their band. He was a peasant from Pokróvsk, near the river Gzhat. When Denísov had come to Pokróvsk at the beginning of his operations and had as usual summoned the village elder and asked him what he knew about the French, the elder, as though shielding himself, had replied, as all village elders did, that he had neither seen nor heard anything of them. But when Denísov explained that his purpose was to kill the French, and asked if no French had strayed that way, the elder replied that some "more-orderers" had really been at their village, but that TíkhonShcherbáty was the only man who dealt with such matters. Denísov had Tíkhon called and, having praised him for his activity, said a few words in the elder's presence about loyalty to the Tsar and the country and the hatred of the French that all sons of the fatherland should cherish.

"We don't do the French any harm," said Tíkhon, evidently frightened by Denísov's words. "We only fooled about with the lads for fun, you know! We killed a score or so of 'more-orderers,' but we did no harm else...."

Next day when Denísov had left Pokróvsk, having quite forgotten about this peasant, it was reported to him that Tíkhon had attached himself to their party and asked to be allowed to remain with it. Denísov gave orders to let him do so.

Tíkhon, who at first did rough work, laying campfires, fetching water, flaying dead horses, and so on, soon showed a great liking and aptitude for partisan warfare. At night he would go out for booty and always brought back French clothing and weapons, and when told to would bring in French captives also. Denísov then relieved him from drudgery and began taking him with him when he went out on expeditions and had him enrolled among the Cossacks.

Tíkhon did not like riding, and always went on foot, never lagging behind the cavalry. He was armed with a musketoon (which he carried rather as a joke), a pike and an ax, which latter he used as a wolf uses its teeth, with equal ease picking fleas out of its fur or crunching thick bones. Tíkhon with equal accuracy would split logs with blows at arm's length, or holding the head of the ax would cut thin little pegs or carve spoons. In Deв́isov's party he held a peculiar and exceptional position. When anything particularly difficult or nasty had to be done—to push a cart out of the mud with one's shoulders, pull a horse out of a swamp by its tail, skin it, slink in among the French, or walk more than thirty miles in a day—everybody pointed laughingly at Tíkhon.

"It won't hurt that devil—he's as strong as a horse!" they said of him.

Once a Frenchman Tíkhon was trying to capture fired a pistol at him and shot him in the fleshy part of the back. That wound (which Tíkhon treated only with internal and external applications of vodka) was the subject of the liveliest jokes by the whole detachment—jokes in which Tíkhon readily joined.

"Hallo, mate! Never again? Gave you a twist?" the Cossacks would banter him. And Tíkhon, purposely writhing and making faces, pretended to be angry and swore at the French with the funniest curses. The only effect of this incident on Tíkhon was that after being wounded he seldom brought in prisoners.

He was the bravest and most useful man in the party. No one found more opportunities for attacking, no one captured or killed more Frenchmen, and consequently he was made the buffoon of all the Cossacks and hussars and willingly accepted that role. Now he had been sent by Deб́isov overnight to Shámshevo to capture a "tongue." But whether because he had not been content to take only one Frenchman or because he had slept through the night, he had crept by day into some bushes right among the French and, as Deб́isov had witnessed from above, had been detected by them.

CHAPTER VI

A fter talking for some time with the *esaul* about next day's attack, which now, seeing how near they were to the French, he seemed to have definitely decided on, Denísov turned his horse and rode back.

"Now, my lad, we'll go and get dwy," he said to Pétya.

As they approached the watchhouse Denísov stopped, peering into the forest. Among the trees a man with long legs and long, swinging arms, wearing a short jacket, bast shoes, and a Kazán hat, was approaching with long, light steps. He had a musketoon over his shoulder and an ax stuck in his girdle. When he espied Denísov he hastily threw something into the bushes, removed his sodden hat by its floppy brim, and approached his commander. It was Tíkhon. His wrinkled and pockmarked face and narrow little eyes beamed with self-satisfied merriment. He lifted his head high and gazed at Denísov as if repressing a laugh.

"Well, where did you disappear to?" inquired Denísov.

"Where did I disappear to? I went to get Frenchmen," answered Tíkhon boldly and hurriedly, in a husky but melodious bass voice.

"Why did you push yourself in there by daylight? You ass! Well, why haven't you taken one?"

"Oh, I took one all right," said Tíkhon.

"Where is he?"

"You see, I took him first thing at dawn," Tíkhon continued, spreading out his flat feet with outturned toes in their bast shoes. "I took him into the forest. Then I see he's no good and think I'll go and fetch a likelier one."

"You see?... What a wogue—it's just as I thought," said Denísov to the *esaul*. "Why didn't you bwing that one?"

"What was the good of bringing him?" Tíkhon interrupted hastily and angrily—"that one wouldn't have done for you. As if I don't know what sort you want!"

"What a bwute you are!... Well?"

"I went for another one," Tíkhon continued, "and I crept like this through the wood and lay down." (He suddenly lay down on his stomach with a supple movement to show how he had done it.) "One turned up and I grabbed him, like this." (He jumped up quickly and lightly.) "'Come along to the colonel,' I said. He starts yelling, and suddenly there were four of them. They rushed at me with their little swords. So I went for them with my ax, this way: 'What are you up to?' says I. 'Christ be with you!'" shouted Tíkhon, waving his arms with an angry scowl and throwing out his chest.

"Yes, we saw from the hill how you took to your heels through the puddles!" said the *esaul*, screwing up his glittering eyes.

Pétya badly wanted to laugh, but noticed that they all refrained from laughing. He turned his eyes rapidly from Tíkhon's face to the *esaul's* and Denísov's, unable to make out what it all meant.

"Don't play the fool!" said Denísov, coughing angrily. "Why didn't you bwing the first one?"

Tíkhon scratched his back with one hand and his head with the other, then suddenly his whole face expanded into a beaming, foolish grin, disclosing a gap where he had lost a tooth (that was why he was called Shcherbáty—the gap-toothed). Denísov smiled, and Pétya burst into a peal of merry laughter in which Tíkhon himself joined.

"Oh, but he was a regular good-for-nothing," said Tíkhon. "The clothes on him—poor stuff! How could I bring him? And so rude, your honor! Why, he says: 'I'm a general's son myself, I won't go!' he says."

"You are a bwute!" said Denísov. "I wanted to question..."

"But I questioned him," said Tíkhon. "He said he didn't know much. 'There are a lot of us,' he says, 'but all poor stuff—only soldiers in name,' he says. 'Shout loud at them,' he says, 'and you'll take them all,'" Tíkhon concluded, looking cheerfully and resolutely into Denísov's eyes.

"I'll give you a hundwed sharp lashes—that'll teach you to play the fool!" said Denísov severely.

"But why are you angry?" remonstrated Tíkhon, "just as if I'd never seen your Frenchmen! Only wait till it gets dark and I'll fetch you any of them you want—three if you like."

"Well, let's go," said Denísov, and rode all the way to the watchhouse in silence and frowning angrily.

Tíkhon followed behind and Pétya heard the Cossacks laughing with him and at him, about some pair of boots he had thrown into the bushes.

When the fit of laughter that had seized him at Tíkhon's words and smile had passed and Pétya realized for a moment that this Tíkhon had killed a man, he felt uneasy. He looked round at the captive drummer boy and felt a pang in his heart. But this uneasiness lasted only a moment. He felt it necessary to hold his head higher, to brace himself, and to question the *esaul* with an air of importance about tomorrow's undertaking, that he might not be unworthy of the company in which he found himself.

The officer who had been sent to inquire met Denísov on the way with the news that Dólokhov was soon coming and that all was well with him.

Denísov at once cheered up and, calling Pétya to him, said: "Well, tell me about yourself."

CHAPTER VII

Pétya, having left his people after their departure from Moscow, joined his regiment and was soon taken as orderly by a general commanding a large guerrilla detachment. From the time he received his commission, and especially since he had joined the active army and taken part in the battle of Vyázma, Pétya had been in a constant state of blissful excitement at being grown-up and in a perpetual ecstatic hurry not to miss any chance to do something really heroic. He was highly delighted with what he saw and experienced in the army, but at the same time it always seemed to him that the really heroic exploits were being performed just where he did not happen to be. And he was always in a hurry to get where he was not.

When on the twenty-first of October his general expressed a wish to send somebody to Denísov's detachment, Pétya begged so piteously to be sent that the general could not refuse. But when dispatching him he recalled Pétya's mad action at the battle of Vyázma, where instead of riding by the road to the place to which he had been sent, he had galloped to the advanced line under the fire of the French and had there twice fired his pistol. So now the general explicitly forbade his taking part in any action whatever of Denísov's. That was why Pétya had blushed and grown confused when Denísov asked him whether he could stay. Before they had ridden to the outskirts of the forest Pétya had considered he must carry out his instructions strictly and return at once. But when he saw the French and saw Tíkhon and learned that there would certainly be an attack that night, he decided, with the rapidity with which young people change their views, that the general, whom he had greatly respected till then, was a rubbishy German, that Denísov was a hero, the *esaul* a hero, and Tíkhon a hero too, and that it would be shameful for him to leave them at a moment of difficulty.

It was already growing dusk when Denísov, Pétya, and the *esaul* rode up to the watchhouse. In the twilight saddled horses could be seen, and Cossacks and hussars who had rigged up rough shelters in the glade and were kindling glowing fires in a hollow of the forest where the French could not see the smoke. In the passage of the small watchhouse a Cossack with sleeves rolled up was chopping some mutton. In the room three officers of Denísov's band were converting a door into a tabletop. Pétya took off his wet clothes, gave them to be dried, and at once began helping the officers to fix up the dinner table.

In ten minutes the table was ready and a napkin spread on it. On the table were vodka, a flask of rum, white bread, roast mutton, and salt.

Sitting at table with the officers and tearing the fat savory mutton with his hands, down which the grease trickled, Pétya was in an ecstatic childish state of love for all men, and consequently of confidence that others loved him in the same way.

"So then what do you think, VasíliDmítrich?" said he to Denísov. "It's all right my staying a day with you?" And not waiting for a reply he answered his own question: "You see I was told to find out—well, I am finding out.... Only do let me into the very... into the chief... I don't want a reward.... But I want..."

Pétya clenched his teeth and looked around, throwing back his head and flourishing his arms.

"Into the vewy chief..." Denísov repeated with a smile.

"Only, please let me command something, so that I may really command..." Pétya went on. "What would it be to you?... Oh, you want a knife?" he said, turning to an officer who wished to cut himself a piece of mutton.

And he handed him his clasp knife. The officer admired it.

"Please keep it. I have several like it," said Pétya, blushing. "Heavens! I was quite forgetting!" he suddenly cried. "I have some raisins, fine ones; you know, seedless ones. We have a new sutler and he has such capital things. I bought ten pounds. I am used to something sweet. Would you like some?..." and Pétya ran out into the passage to his Cossack and brought back some bags which contained about five pounds of raisins. "Have some, gentlemen, have some!"

"You want a coffeepot, don't you?" he asked the *esaul*. "I bought a capital one from our sutler! He has splendid things. And he's very honest, that's the chief thing. I'll be sure to send it to you. Or perhaps your flints are giving out, or are worn out—that happens sometimes, you know. I have brought some with me, here they are"—and he showed a bag—"a hundred flints. I bought them very cheap. Please take as many as you want, or all if you like...."

Then suddenly, dismayed lest he had said too much, Pétya stopped and blushed.

He tried to remember whether he had not done anything else that was foolish. And running over the events of the day he remembered the French drummer boy. "It's capital for us here, but what of him? Where have they put him? Have they fed him? Haven't they hurt his feelings?" he thought. But having caught himself saying too much about the flints, he was now afraid to speak out.

"I might ask," he thought, "but they'll say: 'He's a boy himself and so he pities the boy.' I'll show them tomorrow whether I'm a boy. Will it seem odd if I ask?" Pétya thought. "Well, never mind!" and immediately, blushing and looking anxiously at the officers to see if they appeared ironical, he said:

"May I call in that boy who was taken prisoner and give him something to eat?... Perhaps..."

"Yes, he's a poor little fellow," said Denísov, who evidently saw nothing shameful in this reminder. "Call him in. His name is Vincent Bosse. Have him fetched."

"I'll call him," said Pétya.

"Yes, yes, call him. A poor little fellow," Denísov repeated.

Pétya was standing at the door when Denísov said this. He slipped in between the officers, came close to Denísov, and said:

"Let me kiss you, dear old fellow! Oh, how fine, how splendid!"

And having kissed Denísov he ran out of the hut.

"Bosse! Vincent!" Pétya cried, stopping outside the door.

"Who do you want, sir?" asked a voice in the darkness.

Pétya replied that he wanted the French lad who had been captured that day.

"Ah, Vesénny?" said a Cossack.

Vincent, the boy's name, had already been changed by the Cossacks into *Vesénny* (vernal) and into *Vesénya* by the peasants and soldiers. In both these adaptations the reference to spring (*vesná*) matched the impression made by the young lad.

"He is warming himself there by the bonfire. Ho, Vesénya! Vesénya!—Vesénny!" laughing voices were heard calling to one another in the darkness.

"He's a smart lad," said an hussar standing near Pétya. "We gave him something to eat a while ago. He was awfully hungry!"

The sound of bare feet splashing through the mud was heard in the darkness, and the drummer boy came to the door.

"Ah, c'estvous!" said Pétya. *"Voulez-vous manger? N'ayez pas peur, on ne vousfera pas de mal,"* * he added shyly and affectionately, touching the boy's hand. *"Entrez, entrez."* *(2)

* "Ah, it's you! Do you want something to eat? Don't be afraid, they won't hurt you."

* (2) "Come in, come in."

"Merci, monsieur," * said the drummer boy in a trembling almost childish voice, and he began scraping his dirty feet on the threshold.

* "Thank you, sir."

There were many things Pétya wanted to say to the drummer boy, but did not dare to. He stood irresolutely beside him in the passage. Then in the darkness he took the boy's hand and pressed it.

"Come in, come in!" he repeated in a gentle whisper. "Oh, what can I do for him?" he thought, and opening the door he let the boy pass in first.

When the boy had entered the hut, Pétya sat down at a distance from him, considering it beneath his dignity to pay attention to him. But he fingered the money in his pocket and wondered whether it would seem ridiculous to give some to the drummer boy.

CHAPTER VIII

The arrival of Dólokhov diverted Pétya's attention from the drummer boy, to whom Denísov had had some mutton and vodka given, and whom he had had dressed in a Russian coat so that he might be kept with their band and not sent away with the other prisoners. Pétya had heard in the army many stories of Dólokhov's extraordinary bravery and of his cruelty to the French, so from the moment he entered the hut Pétya did not take his eyes from him, but braced himself up more and more and held his head high, that he might not be unworthy even of such company.

Dólokhov's appearance amazed Pétya by its simplicity.

Denísov wore a Cossack coat, had a beard, had an icon of Nicholas the Wonder-Worker on his breast, and his way of speaking and everything he did indicated his unusual position. But Dólokhov, who in Moscow had worn a Persian costume, had now the appearance of a most correct officer of the Guards. He was clean-shaven and wore a Guardsman's padded coat with an Order of St. George at his buttonhole and a plain forage cap set straight on his head. He took off his wet felt cloak in a corner of the room, and without greeting anyone went up to Denísov and began questioning him about the matter in hand. Denísov told him of the designs the large detachments had on the transport, of the message Pétya had brought, and his own replies to both generals. Then he told him all he knew of the French detachment.

"That's so. But we must know what troops they are and their numbers," said Dólokhov. "It will be necessary to go there. We can't start the affair without knowing for certain how many there are. I like to work accurately. Here now—wouldn't one of these gentlemen like to ride over to the French camp with me? I have brought a spare uniform."

"I, I... I'll go with you!" cried Pétya.

"There's no need for you to go at all," said Denísov, addressing Dólokhov, "and as for him, I won't let him go on any account."

"I like that!" exclaimed Pétya. "Why shouldn't I go?"

"Because it's useless."

"Well, you must excuse me, because... because... I shall go, and that's all. You'll take me, won't you?" he said, turning to Dólokhov.

"Why not?" Dólokhov answered absently, scrutinizing the face of the French drummer boy. "Have you had that youngster with you long?" he asked Denísov.

"He was taken today but he knows nothing. I'm keeping him with me."

"Yes, and where do you put the others?" inquired Dólokhov.

"Where? I send them away and take a weceipt for them," shouted Denísov, suddenly flushing. "And I say boldly that I have not a single man's life on my conscience. Would it be difficult for you to send thirty or thweehundwed men to town under escort, instead of staining—I speak bluntly—staining the honor of a soldier?"

"That kind of amiable talk would be suitable from this young count of sixteen," said Dólokhov with cold irony, "but it's time for you to drop it."

"Why, I've not said anything! I only say that I'll certainly go with you," said Pétya shyly.

"But for you and me, old fellow, it's time to drop these amenities," continued Dólokhov, as if he found particular pleasure in speaking of this subject which irritated Denísov. "Now, why have you kept this lad?" he went on, swaying his head. "Because you are sorry for him! Don't we know those 'receipts' of yours? You send a hundred men away, and thirty get there. The rest either starve or get killed. So isn't it all the same not to send them?"

The *esaul*, screwing up his light-colored eyes, nodded approvingly.

"That's not the point. I'm not going to discuss the matter. I do not wish to take it on my conscience. You say they'll die. All wight. Only not by my fault!"

Dólokhov began laughing.

"Who has told them not to capture me these twenty times over? But if they did catch me they'd string me up to an aspen tree, and with all your chivalry just the same." He paused. "However, we must get to work. Tell the Cossack to fetch my kit. I have two French uniforms in it. Well, are you coming with me?" he asked Pétya.

"I? Yes, yes, certainly!" cried Pétya, blushing almost to tears and glancing at Denísov.

While Dólokhov had been disputing with Denísov what should be done with prisoners, Pétya had once more felt awkward and restless; but again he had no time to grasp fully what they were talking about. "If grown-up, distinguished men think so, it must be necessary and right," thought he. "But above all Denísov must not dare to imagine that I'll obey him and that he can order me about. I will certainly go to the French camp with Dólokhov. If he can, so can I!"

And to all Denísov's persuasions, Pétya replied that he too was accustomed to do everything accurately and not just anyhow, and that he never considered personal danger.

"For you'll admit that if we don't know for sure how many of them there are... hundreds of lives may depend on it, while there are only two of us. Besides, I want to go very much and certainly will go, so don't hinder me," said he. "It will only make things worse...."

CHAPTER IX

Having put on French greatcoats and shakos, Pétya and Dólokhov rode to the clearing from which Denísov had reconnoitered the French camp, and emerging from the forest in pitch darkness they descended into the hollow. On reaching the bottom, Dólokhov told the Cossacks accompanying him to await him there and rode on at a quick trot along the road to the bridge. Pétya, his heart in his mouth with excitement, rode by his side.

"If we're caught, I won't be taken alive! I have a pistol," whispered he.

"Don't talk Russian," said Dólokhov in a hurried whisper, and at that very moment they heard through the darkness the challenge: *"Qui vive?"* * and the click of a musket.

* "Who goes there?"

The blood rushed to Pétya's face and he grasped his pistol.

"Lanciers du 6-me," * replied Dólokhov, neither hastening nor slackening his horse's pace.

* "Lancers of the 6th Regiment."

The black figure of a sentinel stood on the bridge.

"Motd'ordre." *

* "Password."

Dólokhov reined in his horse and advanced at a walk.

"Ditesdonc, le colonel Gérard estici?" * he asked.

* "Tell me, is Colonel Gérard here?"

"Motd'ordre," repeated the sentinel, barring the way and not replying.

"Quand un officier fait sa ronde, les sentinelles ne demandent pas le mot d'ordre..." cried Dólokhov suddenly flaring up and riding straight at the sentinel. *"Je vousdemandesi le colonel estici."* *

* "When an officer is making his round, sentinels don't ask him for the password.... I am asking you if the colonel is here."

And without waiting for an answer from the sentinel, who had stepped aside, Dólokhov rode up the incline at a walk.

Noticing the black outline of a man crossing the road, Dólokhov stopped him and inquired where the commander and officers were. The man, a soldier with a sack over his shoulder, stopped, came close up to Dólokhov's horse, touched it with his hand, and explained simply and in a friendly way that the commander and the officers were higher up the hill to the right in the courtyard of the farm, as he called the landowner's house.

Having ridden up the road, on both sides of which French talk could be heard around the campfires, Dólokhov turned into the courtyard of the landowner's house. Having ridden in, he dismounted and approached a big blazing campfire, around which sat several men talking noisily. Something was boiling in a small cauldron at the edge of the fire and a soldier in a peaked cap and blue overcoat, lit up by the fire, was kneeling beside it stirring its contents with a ramrod.

"Oh, he's a hard nut to crack," said one of the officers who was sitting in the shadow at the other side of the fire.

"He'll make them get a move on, those fellows!" said another, laughing.

Both fell silent, peering out through the darkness at the sound of Dólokhov's and Pétya's steps as they advanced to the fire leading their horses.

"Bonjour, messieurs!" * saidDólokhov loudly and clearly.

* "Good day, gentlemen."

There was a stir among the officers in the shadow beyond the fire, and one tall, long-necked officer, walking round the fire, came up to Dólokhov.

"Is that you, Clément?" he asked. "Where the devil...?" But, noticing his mistake, he broke off short and, with a frown, greeted Dólokhov as a stranger, asking what he could do for him.

Dólokhov said that he and his companion were trying to overtake their regiment, and addressing the company in general asked whether they knew anything of the 6th Regiment. None of them knew anything, and Pétya thought the officers were beginning to look at him and Dólokhov with hostility and suspicion. For some seconds all were silent.

"If you were counting on the evening soup, you have come too late," said a voice from behind the fire with a repressed laugh.

Dólokhov replied that they were not hungry and must push on farther that night.

He handed the horses over to the soldier who was stirring the pot and squatted down on his heels by the fire beside the officer with the long neck. That officer did not take his eyes from Dólokhov and again asked to what regiment he belonged. Dólokhov, as if he had not heard the question, did not reply, but lighting a short French pipe which he took from his pocket began asking the officer in how far the road before them was safe from Cossacks.

"Those brigands are everywhere," replied an officer from behind the fire.

Dólokhov remarked that the Cossacks were a danger only to stragglers such as his companion and himself, "but probably they would not dare to attack large detachments?" he added inquiringly. No one replied.

"Well, now he'll come away," Pétya thought every moment as he stood by the campfire listening to the talk.

But Dólokhov restarted the conversation which had dropped and began putting direct questions as to how many men there were in the battalion, how many battalions, and how many prisoners. Asking about the Russian prisoners with that detachment, Dólokhov said:

"A horrid business dragging these corpses about with one! It would be better to shoot such rabble," and burst into loud laughter, so strange that Pétya thought the French would immediately detect their disguise, and involuntarily took a step back from the campfire.

No one replied a word to Dólokhov's laughter, and a French officer whom they could not see (he lay wrapped in a greatcoat) rose and whispered something to a companion. Dólokhov got up and called to the soldier who was holding their horses.

"Will they bring our horses or not?" thought Pétya, instinctively drawing nearer to Dólokhov.

The horses were brought.

"Good evening, gentlemen," said Dólokhov.

Pétya wished to say "Good night" but could not utter a word. The officers were whispering together. Dólokhov was a long time mounting his horse which would not stand still, then he rode out of the yard at a footpace. Pétya rode beside him, longing to look round to see whether or not the French were running after them, but not daring to.

Coming out onto the road Dólokhov did not ride back across the open country, but through the village. At one spot he stopped and listened. "Do you hear?" he asked. Pétya recognized the sound of Russian voices and saw the dark figures of Russian prisoners round their campfires. When they had descended to the bridge Pétya and Dólokhov rode past the sentinel, who without saying a word paced morosely up and down it, then they descended into the hollow where the Cossacks awaited them.

"Well now, good-by. Tell Denísov, 'at the first shot at daybreak,'" said Dólokhov and was about to ride away, but Pétya seized hold of him.

"Really!" he cried, "you are such a hero! Oh, how fine, how splendid! How I love you!"

"All right, all right!" said Dólokhov. But Pétya did not let go of him and Dólokhov saw through the gloom that Pétya was bending toward him and wanted to kiss him. Dólokhov kissed him, laughed, turned his horse, and vanished into the darkness.

CHAPTER X

Having returned to the watchman's hut, Pétya found Denísov in the passage. He was awaiting Pétya's return in a state of agitation, anxiety, and self-reproach for having let him go.

"Thank God!" he exclaimed. "Yes, thank God!" he repeated, listening to Pétya's rapturous account. "But, devil take you, I haven't slept because of you! Well, thank God. Now lie down. We can still get a nap before morning."

"But... no," said Pétya, "I don't want to sleep yet. Besides I know myself, if I fall asleep it's finished. And then I am used to not sleeping before a battle."

He sat awhile in the hut joyfully recalling the details of his expedition and vividly picturing to himself what would happen next day.

Then, noticing that Denísov was asleep, he rose and went out of doors.

It was still quite dark outside. The rain was over, but drops were still falling from the trees. Near the watchman's hut the black shapes of the Cossacks' shanties and of horses tethered together could be seen. Behind the hut the dark shapes of the two wagons with their horses beside them were discernible, and in the hollow the dying campfire gleamed red. Not all the Cossacks and hussars were asleep; here and there, amid the sounds of falling drops and the munching of the horses near by, could be heard low voices which seemed to be whispering.

Pétya came out, peered into the darkness, and went up to the wagons. Someone was snoring under them, and around them stood saddled horses munching their oats. In the dark Pétya recognized his own horse, which he called "Karabákh" though it was of Ukranian breed, and went up to it.

"Well, Karabákh! We'll do some service tomorrow," said he, sniffing its nostrils and kissing it.

"Why aren't you asleep, sir?" said a Cossack who was sitting under a wagon.

"No, ah... Likhachëv—isn't that your name? Do you know I have only just come back! We've been into the French camp."

And Pétya gave the Cossack a detailed account not only of his ride but also of his object, and why he considered it better to risk his life than to act "just anyhow."

"Well, you should get some sleep now," said the Cossack.

"No, I am used to this," said Pétya. "I say, aren't the flints in your pistols worn out? I brought some with me. Don't you want any? You can have some."

The Cossack bent forward from under the wagon to get a closer look at Pétya.

"Because I am accustomed to doing everything accurately," said Pétya. "Some fellows do things just anyhow, without preparation, and then they're sorry for it afterwards. I don't like that."

"Just so," said the Cossack.

"Oh yes, another thing! Please, my dear fellow, will you sharpen my saber for me? It's got bl..." (Pétya feared to tell a lie, and the saber never had been sharpened.) "Can you do it?"

"Of course I can."

Likhachëv got up, rummaged in his pack, and soon Pétya heard the warlike sound of steel on whetstone. He climbed onto the wagon and sat on its edge. The Cossack was sharpening the saber under the wagon.

"I say! Are the lads asleep?" asked Pétya.

"Some are, and some aren't—like us."

"Well, and that boy?"

"Vesénny? Oh, he's thrown himself down there in the passage. Fast asleep after his fright. He was that glad!"

After that Pétya remained silent for a long time, listening to the sounds. He heard footsteps in the darkness and a black figure appeared.

"What are you sharpening?" asked a man coming up to the wagon.

"Why, this gentleman's saber."

"That's right," said the man, whom Pétya took to be an hussar. "Was the cup left here?"

"There, by the wheel!"

The hussar took the cup.

"It must be daylight soon," said he, yawning, and went away.

Pétya ought to have known that he was in a forest with Denísov's guerrilla band, less than a mile from the road, sitting on a wagon captured from the French beside which horses were tethered, that under it Likhachëv was sitting sharpening a saber for him, that the big dark blotch to the right was the watchman's hut, and the red blotch below to the left was the dying embers of a campfire, that the man who had come for the cup was an hussar who wanted a drink; but he neither knew nor waited to know anything of all this. He was in a fairy kingdom where nothing resembled reality. The big dark blotch might really be the watchman's hut or it might be a cavern leading to the very depths of the earth. Perhaps the red spot was a fire, or it might be the eye of an enormous monster. Perhaps he was really sitting on a wagon, but it might very well be that he was not sitting on a wagon but on a terribly high tower from which, if he fell, he would have to fall for a whole day or a whole month, or go on falling and never reach the bottom. Perhaps it was just the Cossack, Likhachëv, who was sitting under the wagon, but it might be the kindest, bravest, most wonderful, most splendid man in the world, whom no one knew of. It might really have been that the hussar came for water and went back into the hollow, but perhaps he had simply vanished—disappeared altogether and dissolved into nothingness.

Nothing Pétya could have seen now would have surprised him. He was in a fairy kingdom where everything was possible.

He looked up at the sky. And the sky was a fairy realm like the earth. It was clearing, and over the tops of the trees clouds were swiftly sailing as if unveiling the stars. Sometimes it looked as if the clouds were passing, and a clear black sky appeared. Sometimes it seemed as if the black spaces were clouds. Sometimes the sky seemed to be rising high, high overhead, and then it seemed to sink so low that one could touch it with one's hand.

Pétya's eyes began to close and he swayed a little.

The trees were dripping. Quiet talking was heard. The horses neighed and jostled one another. Someone snored.

"Ozheg-zheg, Ozheg-zheg..." hissed the saber against the whetstone, and suddenly Pétya heard an harmonious orchestra playing some unknown, sweetly solemn hymn. Pétya was as musical as Natásha and more so than Nicholas, but had never learned music or thought about it, and so the melody that unexpectedly came to his mind seemed to him particularly fresh and attractive. The music became more and more audible. The melody grew and passed from one instrument to another. And what was played was a fugue—though Pétya had not the least conception of what a fugue is. Each instrument—now resembling a violin and now a horn, but better and clearer than violin or horn—played its own part, and before it had finished the melody merged with another instrument that began almost the same air, and then with a third and a fourth; and they all blended into one and again became separate and again blended, now into solemn church music, now into something dazzlingly brilliant and triumphant.

"Oh—why, that was in a dream!" Pétya said to himself, as he lurched forward. "It's in my ears. But perhaps it's music of my own. Well, go on, my music! Now!..."

He closed his eyes, and, from all sides as if from a distance, sounds fluttered, grew into harmonies, separated, blended, and again all mingled into the same sweet and solemn hymn. "Oh, this is delightful! As much as I like and as I like!" said Pétya to himself. He tried to conduct that enormous orchestra.

"Now softly, softly die away!" and the sounds obeyed him. "Now fuller, more joyful. Still more and more joyful!" And from an unknown depth rose increasingly triumphant sounds. "Now voices join in!" ordered Pétya. And at first from afar he heard men's voices and then women's. The voices grew in harmonious triumphant strength, and Pétya listened to their surpassing beauty in awe and joy.

With a solemn triumphal march there mingled a song, the drip from the trees, and the hissing of the saber, *"Ozheg-zheg-zheg..."* and again the horses jostled one another and neighed, not disturbing the choir but joining in it.

Pétya did not know how long this lasted: he enjoyed himself all the time, wondered at his enjoyment and regretted that there was no one to share it. He was awakened by Likhachëv's kindly voice.

"It's ready, your honor; you can split a Frenchman in half with it!"

Pétya woke up.

"It's getting light, it's really getting light!" he exclaimed.

The horses that had previously been invisible could now be seen to their very tails, and a watery light showed itself through the bare branches. Pétya shook himself, jumped up, took a ruble from his pocket and gave it to Likhachëv; then he flourished the saber, tested it, and sheathed it. The Cossacks were untying their horses and tightening their saddle girths.

"And here's the commander," said Likhachëv.

Denísov came out of the watchman's hut and, having called Pétya, gave orders to get ready.

CHAPTER XI

The men rapidly picked out their horses in the semidarkness, tightened their saddle girths, and formed companies. Denísov stood by the watchman's hut giving final orders. The infantry of the detachment passed along the road and quickly disappeared amid the trees in the mist of early dawn, hundreds of feet splashing through the mud. The *esaul* gave some orders to his men. Pétya held his horse by the bridle, impatiently awaiting the order to mount. His face, having been bathed in cold water, was all aglow, and his eyes were particularly brilliant. Cold shivers ran down his spine and his whole body pulsed rhythmically.

"Well, is ev'wythingweady?" asked Denísov. "Bwing the horses."

The horses were brought. Denísov was angry with the Cossack because the saddle girths were too slack, reproved him, and mounted. Pétya put his foot in the stirrup. His horse by habit made as if to nip his leg, but Pétya leaped quickly into the saddle unconscious of his own weight and, turning to look at the hussars starting in the darkness behind him, rode up to Denísov.

"VasíliDmítrich, entrust me with some commission! Please... for God's sake...!" said he.

Denísov seemed to have forgotten Pétya's very existence. He turned to glance at him.

"I ask one thing of you," he said sternly, "to obey me and not shove yourself forward anywhere."

He did not say another word to Pétya but rode in silence all the way. When they had come to the edge of the forest it was noticeably growing light over the field. Denísov talked in whispers with the *esaul* and the Cossacks rode past Pétya and Denísov. When they had all ridden by, Denísov touched his horse and rode down the hill. Slipping onto their haunches and sliding, the horses descended with their riders into the ravine. Pétya rode beside Denísov, the pulsation of his body constantly increasing. It was getting lighter and lighter, but the mist still hid distant objects. Having reached the valley, Denísov looked back and nodded to a Cossack beside him.

"The signal!" said he.

The Cossack raised his arm and a shot rang out. In an instant the tramp of horses galloping forward was heard, shouts came from various sides, and then more shots.

At the first sound of trampling hoofs and shouting, Pétya lashed his horse and loosening his rein galloped forward, not heeding Denísov who shouted at him. It seemed to Pétya that at the moment the shot was fired it suddenly became as bright as noon. He galloped to the bridge. Cossacks were galloping along the road in front of him. On the bridge he collided with a Cossack who had fallen behind, but he galloped on. In front of him soldiers, probably Frenchmen, were running from right to left across the road. One of them fell in the mud under his horse's feet.

Cossacks were crowding about a hut, busy with something. From the midst of that crowd terrible screams arose. Pétya galloped up, and the first thing he saw was the pale face and trembling jaw of a Frenchman, clutching the handle of a lance that had been aimed at him.

"Hurrah!... Lads!... ours!" shouted Pétya, and giving rein to his excited horse he galloped forward along the village street.

He could hear shooting ahead of him. Cossacks, hussars, and ragged Russian prisoners, who had come running from both sides of the road, were shouting something loudly and incoherently. A gallant-looking Frenchman, in a blue overcoat, capless, and with a frowning red face, had been defending himself against the hussars.

When Pétya galloped up the Frenchman had already fallen. "Too late again!" flashed through Pétya's mind and he galloped on to the place from which the rapid firing could be heard. The shots came from the yard of the landowner's house he had visited the night before with Dólokhov. The French were making a stand there behind a wattle fence in a garden thickly overgrown with bushes and were firing at the Cossacks who crowded at the gateway. Through the smoke, as he approached the gate, Pétya saw Dólokhov, whose face was of a pale-greenish tint, shouting to his men. "Go round! Wait for the infantry!" he exclaimed as Pétya rode up to him.

"Wait?... Hurrah-ah-ah!" shouted Pétya, and without pausing a moment galloped to the place whence came the sounds of firing and where the smoke was thickest.

A volley was heard, and some bullets whistled past, while others plashed against something. The Cossacks and Dólokhov galloped after Pétya into the gateway of the courtyard. In the dense wavering smoke some of the French threw down their arms and ran out of the bushes to meet the Cossacks, while others ran down the hill toward the pond. Pétya was galloping along the courtyard, but instead of holding the reins he waved both his arms about rapidly and strangely, slipping farther and farther to one side in his saddle. His horse, having galloped up to a campfire that was smoldering in the morning light, stopped suddenly, and Pétya fell heavily on to the wet ground. The Cossacks saw that his arms and legs jerked rapidly though his head was quite motionless. A bullet had pierced his skull.

After speaking to the senior French officer, who came out of the house with a white handkerchief tied to his sword and announced that they surrendered, Dólokhov dismounted and went up to Pétya, who lay motionless with outstretched arms.

"Done for!" he said with a frown, and went to the gate to meet Denísov who was riding toward him.

"Killed?" cried Denísov, recognizing from a distance the unmistakably lifeless attitude—very familiar to him—in which Pétya's body was lying.

"Done for!" repeated Dólokhov as if the utterance of these words afforded him pleasure, and he went quickly up to the prisoners, who were surrounded by Cossacks who had hurried up. "We won't take them!" he called out to Denísov.

Denísov did not reply; he rode up to Pétya, dismounted, and with trembling hands turned toward himself the bloodstained, mud-bespattered face which had already gone white.

"I am used to something sweet. Raisins, fine ones... take them all!" he recalled Pétya's words. And the Cossacks looked round in surprise at the sound, like the yelp of a dog, with which Denísov turned away, walked to the wattle fence, and seized hold of it.

Among the Russian prisoners rescued by Denísov and Dólokhov was Pierre Bezúkhov.

CHAPTER XII

During the whole of their march from Moscow no fresh orders had been issued by the French authorities concerning the party of prisoners among whom was Pierre. On the twenty-second of October that party was no longer with the same troops and baggage trains with which it had left Moscow. Half the wagons laden with hardtack that had traveled the first stages with them had been captured by Cossacks, the other half had gone on ahead. Not one of those dismounted cavalrymen who had marched in front of the prisoners was left; they had all disappeared. The artillery the prisoners had seen in front of them during the first days was now replaced by Marshal Junot's enormous baggage train, convoyed by Westphalians. Behind the prisoners came a cavalry baggage train.

From Vyázma onwards the French army, which had till then moved in three columns, went on as a single group. The symptoms of disorder that Pierre had noticed at their first halting place after leaving Moscow had now reached the utmost limit.

The road along which they moved was bordered on both sides by dead horses; ragged men who had fallen behind from various regiments continually changed about, now joining the moving column, now again lagging behind it.

Several times during the march false alarms had been given and the soldiers of the escort had raised their muskets, fired, and run headlong, crushing one another, but had afterwards reassembled and abused each other for their causeless panic.

These three groups traveling together—the cavalry stores, the convoy of prisoners, and Junot's baggage train—still constituted a separate and united whole, though each of the groups was rapidly melting away.

Of the artillery baggage train which had consisted of a hundred and twenty wagons, not more than sixty now remained; the rest had been captured or left behind. Some of Junot's wagons also had been captured or abandoned. Three wagons had been raided and robbed by stragglers from Davout's corps. From the talk of the Germans Pierre learned that a larger guard had been allotted to that baggage train than to the prisoners, and that one of their comrades, a German soldier, had been shot by the marshal's own order because a silver spoon belonging to the marshal had been found in his possession.

The group of prisoners had melted away most of all. Of the three hundred and thirty men who had set out from Moscow fewer than a hundred now remained. The prisoners were more burdensome to the escort than even the cavalry saddles or Junot's baggage. They understood that the saddles and Junot's spoon might be of some use, but that cold and hungry soldiers should have to stand and guard equally cold and hungry Russians who froze and lagged behind on the road (in which case the order was to shoot them) was not merely incomprehensible but revolting. And the escort, as if afraid, in the grievous condition they themselves were in, of giving way to the pity they felt for the prisoners and so rendering their own plight still worse, treated them with particular moroseness and severity.

At Dorogobúzh while the soldiers of the convoy, after locking the prisoners in a stable, had gone off to pillage their own stores, several of the soldier prisoners tunneled under the wall and ran away, but were recaptured by the French and shot.

The arrangement adopted when they started, that the officer prisoners should be kept separate from the rest, had long since been abandoned. All who could walk went together, and after the third stage Pierre had rejoinedKarataev and the gray-blue bandy-legged dog that had chosen Karataev for its master.

On the third day after leaving Moscow Karataev again fell ill with the fever he had suffered from in the hospital in Moscow, and as he grew gradually weaker Pierre kept away from him. Pierre did not know why, but since Karataev had begun to grow weaker it had cost him an effort to go near him. When he did so and heard the subdued moaning with which Karataev generally lay down at the halting places, and when he smelled the odor emanating from him which was now stronger than before, Pierre moved farther away and did not think about him.

While imprisoned in the shed Pierre had learned not with his intellect but with his whole being, by life itself, that man is created for happiness, that happiness is within him, in the satisfaction of simple human needs, and that all unhappiness arises not from privation but from superfluity. And now during these last three weeks of the march he had learned still another new, consolatory truth—that nothing in this world is terrible. He had learned that as there is no condition in which man can be happy and entirely free, so there is no condition in which he need be unhappy and lack freedom. He learned that suffering and freedom have their limits and that those limits are very near together; that the person in a bed of roses with one crumpled petal suffered as keenly as he now, sleeping on the bare damp earth with one side growing chilled while the other was warming; and that when he had put on tight dancing shoes he had suffered just as he did now when he walked with bare feet that were covered with sores— his footgear having long since fallen to pieces. He discovered that when he had married his wife—of his own free will as it had seemed to him—he had been no more free than now when they locked him up at night in a stable. Of all that he himself subsequently termed his sufferings, but which at the time he scarcely felt, the worst was the state of his bare, raw, and scab-covered feet. (The horseflesh was appetizing and nourishing, the saltpeterflavor of the gunpowder they used instead of salt was even pleasant; there was no great cold, it was always warm walking in the daytime, and at night there were the campfires; the lice that devoured him warmed his body.) The one thing that was at first hard to bear was his feet.

After the second day's march Pierre, having examined his feet by the campfire, thought it would be impossible to walk on them; but when everybody got up he went along, limping, and, when he had warmed up, walked without feeling the pain, though at night his feet were more terrible to look at than before. However, he did not look at them now, but thought of other things.

Only now did Pierre realize the full strength of life in man and the saving power he has of transferring his attention from one thing to another, which is like the safety valve of a boiler that allows superfluous steam to blow off when the pressure exceeds a certain limit.

He did not see and did not hear how they shot the prisoners who lagged behind, though more than a hundred perished in that way. He did not think of Karatáev who grew weaker every day and evidently would soon have to share that fate. Still less did Pierre think about himself. The harder his position became and the more terrible the future, the more independent of that position in which he found himself were the joyful and comforting thoughts, memories, and imaginings that came to him.

CHAPTER XIII

At midday on the twenty-second of October Pierre was going uphill along the muddy, slippery road, looking at his feet and at the roughness of the way. Occasionally he glanced at the familiar crowd around him and then again at his feet. The former and the latter were alike familiar and his own. The blue-gray bandy legged dog ran merrily along the side of the road, sometimes in proof of its agility and self-satisfaction lifting one hind leg and hopping along on three, and then again going on all four and rushing to bark at the crows that sat on the carrion. The dog was merrier and sleeker than it had been in Moscow. All around lay the flesh of different animals—from men to horses—in various stages of decomposition; and as the wolves were kept off by the passing men the dog could eat all it wanted.

It had been raining since morning and had seemed as if at any moment it might cease and the sky clear, but after a short break it began raining harder than before. The saturated road no longer absorbed the water, which ran along the ruts in streams.

Pierre walked along, looking from side to side, counting his steps in threes, and reckoning them off on his fingers. Mentally addressing the rain, he repeated: "Now then, now then, go on! Pelt harder!"

It seemed to him that he was thinking of nothing, but far down and deep within him his soul was occupied with something important and comforting. This something was a most subtle spiritual deduction from a conversation with Karatáev the day before.

At their yesterday's halting place, feeling chilly by a dying campfire, Pierre had got up and gone to the next one, which was burning better. There PlatónKaratáev was sitting covered up—head and all—with his greatcoat as if it were a vestment, telling the soldiers in his effective and pleasant though now feeble voice a story Pierre knew. It was already past midnight, the hour when Karatáev was usually free of his fever and particularly lively. When Pierre reached the fire and heard Platón's voice enfeebled by illness, and saw his pathetic face brightly lit up by the blaze, he felt a painful prick at his heart. His feeling of pity for this man frightened him and he wished to go away, but there was no other fire, and Pierre sat down, trying not to look at Platón.

"Well, how are you?" he asked.

"How am I? If we grumble at sickness, God won't grant us death," replied Platón, and at once resumed the story he had begun.

"And so, brother," he continued, with a smile on his pale emaciated face and a particularly happy light in his eyes, "you see, brother..."

Pierre had long been familiar with that story. Karatáev had told it to him alone some half-dozen times and always with a specially joyful emotion. But well as he knew it, Pierre now listened to that tale as to something new, and the quiet rapture Karatáev evidently felt as he told it communicated itself also to Pierre. The story was of an old merchant who lived a good and God-fearing life with his family, and who went once to the Nízhni fair with a companion—a rich merchant.

Having put up at an inn they both went to sleep, and next morning his companion was found robbed and with his throat cut. A bloodstained knife was found under the old merchant's pillow. He was tried, knouted, and his nostrils having been torn off, "all in due form" as Karatáev put it, he was sent to hard labor in Siberia.

"And so, brother" (it was at this point that Pierre came up), "ten years or more passed by. The old man was living as a convict, submitting as he should and doing no wrong. Only he prayed to God for death. Well, one night the convicts were gathered just as we are, with the old man among them. And they began telling what each was suffering for, and how they had sinned against God. One told how he had taken a life, another had taken two, a third had set a house on fire, while another had simply been a vagrant and had done nothing. So they asked the old man: 'What are you being punished for, Daddy?'—'I, my dear brothers,' said he, 'am being punished for my own and other men's sins. But I have not killed anyone or taken anything that was not mine, but have only helped my poorer brothers. I was a merchant, my dear brothers, and had much property. 'And he went on to tell them all about it in due order. 'I don't grieve for myself,' he says, 'God, it seems, has chastened me. Only I am sorry for my old wife and the children,' and the old man began to weep. Now it happened that in the group was the very man who had killed the other merchant. 'Where did it happen, Daddy?' he said. 'When, and in what month?' He asked all about it and his heart began to ache. So he comes up to the old man like this, and falls down at his feet! 'You are perishing because of me, Daddy,' he says. 'It's quite true, lads, that this man,' he says, 'is being tortured innocently and for nothing! I,' he says, 'did that deed, and I put the knife under your head while you were asleep. Forgive me, Daddy,' he says, 'for Christ's sake!'"

Karatáev paused, smiling joyously as he gazed into the fire, and he drew the logs together.

"And the old man said, 'God will forgive you, we are all sinners in His sight. I suffer for my own sins,' and he wept bitter tears. Well, and what do you think, dear friends?" Karatáev continued, his face brightening more and more with a rapturous smile as if what he now had to tell contained the chief charm and the whole meaning of his story: "What do you think, dear fellows? That murderer confessed to the authorities. 'I have taken six lives,' he says (he was a great sinner), 'but what I am most sorry for is this old man. Don't let him suffer because of me.' So he confessed and it was all written down and the papers sent off in due form. The place was a long way off, and while they were judging, what with one thing and another, filling in the papers all in due form—the authorities I mean—time passed. The affair reached the Tsar. After a while the Tsar's decree came: to set the merchant free and give him a compensation that had been awarded. The paper arrived and they began to look for the old man. 'Where is the old man who has been suffering innocently and in vain? A paper has come from the Tsar!' so they began looking for him," here Karatáev's lower jaw trembled, "but God had already forgiven him— he was dead! That's how it was, dear fellows!" Karatáev concluded and sat for a long time silent, gazing before him with a smile.

And Pierre's soul was dimly but joyfully filled not by the story itself but by its mysterious significance: by the rapturous joy that lit up Karatáev's face as he told it, and the mystic significance of that joy.

CHAPTER XIV

"À vos places!" * suddenly cried a voice.

* "To your places."

A pleasant feeling of excitement and an expectation of something joyful and solemn was aroused among the soldiers of the convoy and the prisoners. From all sides came shouts of command, and from the left came smartly dressed cavalrymen on good horses, passing the prisoners at a trot. The expression on all faces showed the tension people feel at the approach of those in authority. The prisoners thronged together and were pushed off the road. The convoy formed up.

"The Emperor! The Emperor! The Marshal! The Duke!" and hardly had the sleek cavalry passed, before a carriage drawn by six gray horses rattled by. Pierre caught a glimpse of a man in a three-cornered hat with a tranquil look on his handsome, plump, white face. It was one of the marshals. His eye fell on Pierre's large and striking figure, and in the expression with which he frowned and looked away Pierre thought he detected sympathy and a desire to conceal that sympathy.

The general in charge of the stores galloped after the carriage with a red and frightened face, whipping up his skinny horse. Several officers formed a group and some soldiers crowded round them. Their faces all looked excited and worried.

"What did he say? What did he say?" Pierre heard them ask.

While the marshal was passing, the prisoners had huddled together in a crowd, and Pierre saw Karatáev whom he had not yet seen that morning. He sat in his short overcoat leaning against a birch tree. On his face, besides the look of joyful emotion it had worn yesterday while telling the tale of the merchant who suffered innocently, there was now an expression of quiet solemnity.

Karatáev looked at Pierre with his kindly round eyes now filled with tears, evidently wishing him to come near that he might say something to him. But Pierre was not sufficiently sure of himself. He made as if he did not notice that look and moved hastily away.

When the prisoners again went forward Pierre looked round. Karatáev was still sitting at the side of the road under the birch tree and two Frenchmen were talking over his head. Pierre did not look round again but went limping up the hill.

From behind, where Karatáev had been sitting, came the sound of a shot. Pierre heard it plainly, but at that moment he remembered that he had not yet finished reckoning up how many stages still remained to Smolénsk—a calculation he had begun before the marshal went by. And he again started reckoning. Two French soldiers ran past Pierre, one of whom carried a lowered and smoking gun. They both looked pale, and in the expression on their faces—one of them glanced timidly at Pierre—there was something resembling what he had seen on the face of the young soldier at the execution. Pierre looked at the soldier and remembered that, two days before, that man had burned his shirt while drying it at the fire and how they had laughed at him.

Behind him, where Karatáev had been sitting, the dog began to howl. "What a stupid beast! Why is it howling?" thought Pierre.

His comrades, the prisoner soldiers walking beside him, avoided looking back at the place where the shot had been fired and the dog was howling, just as Pierre did, but there was a set look on all their faces.

CHAPTER XV

The stores, the prisoners, and the marshal's baggage train stopped at the village of Shámshevo. The men crowded together round the campfires. Pierre went up to the fire, ate some roast horseflesh, lay down with his back to the fire, and immediately fell asleep. He again slept as he had done at Mozháysk after the battle of Borodinó.

Again real events mingled with dreams and again someone, he or another, gave expression to his thoughts, and even to the same thoughts that had been expressed in his dream at Mozháysk.

"Life is everything. Life is God. Everything changes and moves and that movement is God. And while there is life there is joy in consciousness of the divine. To love life is to love God. Harder and more blessed than all else is to love this life in one's sufferings, in innocent sufferings."

"Karatáev!" came to Pierre's mind.

And suddenly he saw vividly before him a long-forgotten, kindly old man who had given him geography lessons in Switzerland. "Wait a bit," said the old man, and showed Pierre a globe. This globe was alive—a vibrating ball without fixed dimensions. Its whole surface consisted of drops closely pressed together, and all these drops moved and changed places, sometimes several of them merging into one, sometimes one dividing into many. Each drop tried to spread out and occupy as much space as possible, but others striving to do the same compressed it, sometimes destroyed it, and sometimes merged with it.

"That is life," said the old teacher.

"How simple and clear it is," thought Pierre. "How is it I did not know it before?"

"God is in the midst, and each drop tries to expand so as to reflect Him to the greatest extent. And it grows, merges, disappears from the surface, sinks to the depths, and again emerges. There now, Karatáev has spread out and disappeared. Do you understand, my child?" said the teacher.

"Do you understand, damn you?" shouted a voice, and Pierre woke up.

He lifted himself and sat up. A Frenchman who had just pushed a Russian soldier away was squatting by the fire, engaged in roasting a piece of meat stuck on a ramrod. His sleeves were rolled up and his sinewy, hairy, red hands with their short fingers deftly turned the ramrod. His brown morose face with frowning brows was clearly visible by the glow of the charcoal.

"It's all the same to him," he muttered, turning quickly to a soldier who stood behind him. "Brigand! Get away!"

And twisting the ramrod he looked gloomily at Pierre, who turned away and gazed into the darkness. A prisoner, the Russian soldier the Frenchman had pushed away, was sitting near the fire patting something with his hand. Looking more closely Pierre recognized the blue-gray dog, sitting beside the soldier, wagging its tail.

"Ah, he's come?" said Pierre. "And Plat—" he began, but did not finish.

Suddenly and simultaneously a crowd of memories awoke in his fancy—of the look Platón had given him as he sat under the tree, of the shot heard from that spot, of the dog's howl, of the guilty faces of the two Frenchmen as they ran past him, of the lowered and smoking gun, and of Karatáev's absence at this halt—and he was on the point of realizing that Karatáev had been killed, but just at that instant, he knew not why, the recollection came to his mind of a summer evening he had spent with a beautiful Polish lady on the veranda of his house in Kiev. And without linking up the events of the day or drawing a conclusion from them, Pierre closed his eyes, seeing a vision of the country in summertime mingled with memories of bathing and of the liquid, vibrating globe, and he sank into water so that it closed over his head.

Before sunrise he was awakened by shouts and loud and rapid firing. French soldiers were running past him.

"The Cossacks!" one of them shouted, and a moment later a crowd of Russians surrounded Pierre.

For a long time he could not understand what was happening to him. All around he heard his comrades sobbing with joy.

"Brothers! Dear fellows! Darlings!" old soldiers exclaimed, weeping, as they embraced Cossacks and hussars.

The hussars and Cossacks crowded round the prisoners; one offered them clothes, another boots, and a third bread. Pierre sobbed as he sat among them and could not utter a word. He hugged the first soldier who approached him, and kissed him, weeping.

Dólokhov stood at the gate of the ruined house, letting a crowd of disarmed Frenchmen pass by. The French, excited by all that had happened, were talking loudly among themselves, but as they passed Dólokhov who gently switched his boots with his whip and watched them with cold glassy eyes that boded no good, they became silent. On the opposite side stood Dólokhov's Cossack, counting the prisoners and marking off each hundred with a chalk line on the gate.

"How many?" Dólokhov asked the Cossack.

"The second hundred," replied the Cossack.

"*Filez, filez!*" * Dólokhov kept saying, having adopted this expression from the French, and when his eyes met those of the prisoners they flashed with a cruel light.

* "Get along, get along!"

Denísov, bareheaded and with a gloomy face, walked behind some Cossacks who were carrying the body of PétyaRostóv to a hole that had been dug in the garden.

CHAPTER XVI

After the twenty-eighth of October when the frosts began, the flight of the French assumed a still more tragic character, with men freezing, or roasting themselves to death at the campfires, while carriages with people dressed in furs continued to drive past, carrying away the property that had been stolen by the Emperor, kings, and dukes; but the process of the flight and disintegration of the French army went on essentially as before.

From Moscow to Vyázma the French army of seventy-three thousand men not reckoning the Guards (who did nothing during the whole war but pillage) was reduced to thirty-six thousand, though not more than five thousand had fallen in battle. From this beginning the succeeding terms of the progression could be determined mathematically. The French army melted away and perished at the same rate from Moscow to Vyázma, from Vyázma to Smolénsk, from Smolénsk to the Berëzina, and from the Berëzina to Vílna—independently of the greater or lesser intensity of the cold, the pursuit, the barring of the way, or any other particular conditions. Beyond Vyázma the French army instead of moving in three columns huddled together into one mass, and so went on to the end. Berthier wrote to his Emperor (we know how far commanding officers allow themselves to diverge from the truth in describing the condition of an army) and this is what he said:

I deem it my duty to report to Your Majesty the condition of the various corps I have had occasion to observe during different stages of the last two or three days' march. They are almost disbanded. Scarcely a quarter of the soldiers remain with the standards of their regiments, the others go off by themselves in different directions hoping to find food and escape discipline. In general they regard Smolénsk as the place where they hope to recover. During the last few days many of the men have been seen to throw away their cartridges and their arms. In such a state of affairs, whatever your ultimate plans may be, the interest of Your Majesty's service demands that the army should be rallied at Smolénsk and should first of all be freed from ineffectives, such as dismounted cavalry, unnecessary baggage, and artillery material that is no longer in proportion to the present forces. The soldiers, who are worn out with hunger and fatigue, need these supplies as well as a few days' rest. Many have died these last days on the road or at the bivouacs. This state of things is continually becoming worse and makes one fear that unless a prompt remedy is applied the troops will no longer be under control in case of an engagement.

November 9: twenty miles from Smolénsk.

After staggering into Smolénsk which seemed to them a promised land, the French, searching for food, killed one another, sacked their own stores, and when everything had been plundered fled farther.

They all went without knowing whither or why they were going. Still less did that genius, Napoleon, know it, for no one issued any orders to him. But still he and those about him retained their old habits: wrote commands, letters, reports, and orders of the day; called one another *sire, mon cousin, prince d'Eckmühl, roi de Naples,* and so on. But these orders and reports were only on paper, nothing in them was acted upon for they could not be carried out, and though they entitled one another Majesties, Highnesses, or Cousins, they all felt that they were miserable wretches who had done much evil for which they had now to pay. And though they pretended to be concerned about the army, each was thinking only of himself and of how to get away quickly and save himself.

CHAPTER XVII

The movements of the Russian and French armies during the campaign from Moscow back to the Niemen were like those in a game of Russian blindman's buff, in which two players are blindfolded and one of them occasionally rings a little bell to inform the catcher of his whereabouts. First he rings his bell fearlessly, but when he gets into a tight place he runs away as quietly as he can, and often thinking to escape runs straight into his opponent's arms.

At first while they were still moving along the Kalúga road, Napoleon's armies made their presence known, but later when they reached the Smolénsk road they ran holding the clapper of their bell tight—and often thinking they were escaping ran right into the Russians.

Owing to the rapidity of the French flight and the Russian pursuit and the consequent exhaustion of the horses, the chief means of approximately ascertaining the enemy's position—by cavalry scouting—was not available. Besides, as a result of the frequent and rapid change of position by each army, even what information was obtained could not be delivered in time. If news was received one day that the enemy had been in a certain position the day before, by the third day when something could have been done, that army was already two days' march farther on and in quite another position.

One army fled and the other pursued. Beyond Smolénsk there were several different roads available for the French, and one would have thought that during their stay of four days they might have learned where the enemy was, might have arranged some more advantageous plan and undertaken something new. But after a four days' halt the mob, with no maneuvers or plans, again began running along the beaten track, neither to the right nor to the left but along the old—the worst—road, through Krásnoe and Orshá.

Expecting the enemy from behind and not in front, the French separated in their flight and spread out over a distance of twenty-four hours. In front of them all fled the Emperor, then the kings, then the dukes. The Russian army, expecting Napoleon to take the road to the right beyond the Dnieper—which was the only reasonable thing for him to do—themselves turned to the right and came out onto the highroad at Krásnoe. And here as in a game of blindman's buff the French ran into our vanguard. Seeing their enemy unexpectedly the French fell into confusion and stopped short from the sudden fright, but then they resumed their flight, abandoning their comrades who were farther behind. Then for three days separate portions of the French army—first Murat's (the vice-king's), then Davout's, and then Ney's—ran, as it were, the gauntlet of the Russian army. They abandoned one another, abandoned all their heavy baggage, their artillery, and half their men, and fled, getting past the Russians by night by making semicircles to the right.

Ney, who came last, had been busying himself blowing up the walls of Smolénsk which were in nobody's way, because despite the unfortunate plight of the French or because of it, they wished to punish the floor against which they had hurt themselves. Ney, who had had a corps of ten thousand men, reached Napoleon at Orshá with only one thousand men left, having abandoned all the rest and all his cannon, and having crossed the Dnieper at night by stealth at a wooded spot.

From Orshá they fled farther along the road to Vílna, still playing at blindman's buff with the pursuing army. At the Berëzina they again became disorganized, many were drowned and many surrendered, but those who got across the river fled farther. Their supreme chief donned a fur coat and, having seated himself in a sleigh, galloped on alone, abandoning his companions. The others who could do so drove away too, leaving those who could not to surrender or die.

CHAPTER XVIII

This campaign consisted in a flight of the French during which they did all they could to destroy themselves. From the time they turned onto the Kalúga road to the day their leader fled from the army, none of the movements of the crowd had any sense. So one might have thought that regarding this period of the campaign the historians, who attributed the actions of the mass to the will of one man, would have found it impossible to make the story of the retreat fit their theory. But no! Mountains of books have been written by the historians about this campaign, and everywhere are described Napoleon's arrangements, the maneuvers, and his profound plans which guided the army, as well as the military genius shown by his marshals.

The retreat from Málo-Yaroslávets when he had a free road into a well-supplied district and the parallel road was open to him along which Kutúzov afterwards pursued him—this unnecessary retreat along a devastated road—is explained to us as being due to profound considerations. Similarly profound considerations are given for his retreat from Smolénsk to Orshá. Then his heroism at Krásnoe is described, where he is reported to have been prepared to accept battle and take personal command, and to have walked about with a birch stick and said:

"J'aiassez fait l'empereur; il est temps de faire le général," * but nevertheless immediately ran away again, abandoning to its fate the scattered fragments of the army he left behind.

* "I have acted the Emperor long enough; it is time to act the general."

Then we are told of the greatness of soul of the marshals, especially of Ney—a greatness of soul consisting in this: that he made his way by night around through the forest and across the Dnieper and escaped to Orshá, abandoning standards, artillery, and nine tenths of his men.

And lastly, the final departure of the great Emperor from his heroic army is presented to us by the historians as something great and characteristic of genius. Even that final running away, described in ordinary language as the lowest depth of baseness which every child is taught to be ashamed of—even that act finds justification in the historians' language.

When it is impossible to stretch the very elastic threads of historical ratiocination any farther, when actions are clearly contrary to all that humanity calls right or even just, the historians produce a saving conception of "greatness." "Greatness," it seems, excludes the standards of right and wrong. For the "great" man nothing is wrong, there is no atrocity for which a "great" man can be blamed.

"*C'est grand!*" * say the historians, and there no longer exists either good or evil but only "*grand*" and "not *grand*." *Grand* is good, not *grand* is bad. *Grand* is the characteristic, in their conception, of some special animals called "heroes." And Napoleon, escaping home in a warm fur coat and leaving to perish those who were not merely his comrades but were (in his opinion) men he had brought there, feels *que c'est grand,* *(2) and his soul is tranquil.

* "It is great."

* (2) That it is great.

"*Du sublime* (he saw something sublime in himself) *au ridicule il n'y a qu'un pas,*" * said he. And the whole world for fifty years has been repeating: "*Sublime! Grand! Napoléon le Grand!*" *Du sublime au ridicule il n'y a qu'un pas.*

* "From the sublime to the ridiculous is but a step."

And it occurs to no one that to admit a greatness not commensurable with the standard of right and wrong is merely to admit one's own nothingness and immeasurable meanness.

For us with the standard of good and evil given us by Christ, no human actions are incommensurable. And there is no greatness where simplicity, goodness, and truth are absent.

CHAPTER XIX

What Russian, reading the account of the last part of the campaign of 1812, has not experienced an uncomfortable feeling of regret, dissatisfaction, and perplexity? Who has not asked himself how it is that the French were not all captured or destroyed when our three armies surrounded them in superior numbers, when the disordered French, hungry and freezing, surrendered in crowds, and when (as the historians relate) the aim of the Russians was to stop the French, to cut them off, and capture them all?

How was it that the Russian army, which when numerically weaker than the French had given battle at Borodinó, did not achieve its purpose when it had surrounded the French on three sides and when its aim was to capture them? Can the French be so enormously superior to us that when we had surrounded them with superior forces we could not beat them? How could that happen?

History (or what is called by that name) replying to these questions says that this occurred because Kutúzov and Tormásov and Chichagóv, and this man and that man, did not execute such and such maneuvers....

But why did they not execute those maneuvers? And why if they were guilty of not carrying out a prearranged plan were they not tried and punished? But even if we admitted that Kutúzov, Chichagóv, and others were the cause of the Russian failures, it is still incomprehensible why, the position of the Russian army being what it was at Krásnoe and at the Berëzina (in both cases we had superior forces), the French army with its marshals, kings, and Emperor was not captured, if that was what the Russians aimed at.

The explanation of this strange fact given by Russian military historians (to the effect that Kutúzov hindered an attack) is unfounded, for we know that he could not restrain the troops from attacking at Vyázma and Tarútino.

Why was the Russian army—which with inferior forces had withstood the enemy in full strength at Borodinó—defeated at Krásnoe and the Berëzina by the disorganized crowds of the French when it was numerically superior?

If the aim of the Russians consisted in cutting off and capturing Napoleon and his marshals—and that aim was not merely frustrated but all attempts to attain it were most shamefully baffled—then this last period of the campaign is quite rightly considered by the French to be a series of victories, and quite wrongly considered victorious by Russian historians.

The Russian military historians in so far as they submit to claims of logic must admit that conclusion, and in spite of their lyrical rhapsodies about valor, devotion, and so forth, must reluctantly admit that the French retreat from Moscow was a series of victories for Napoleon and defeats for Kutúzov.

But putting national vanity entirely aside one feels that such a conclusion involves a contradiction, since the series of French victories brought the French complete destruction, while the series of Russian defeats led to the total destruction of their enemy and the liberation of their country.

The source of this contradiction lies in the fact that the historians studying the events from the letters of the sovereigns and the generals, from memoirs, reports, projects, and so forth, have attributed to this last period of the war of 1812 an aim that never existed, namely that of cutting off and capturing Napoleon with his marshals and his army.

There never was or could have been such an aim, for it would have been senseless and its attainment quite impossible.

It would have been senseless, first because Napoleon's disorganized army was flying from Russia with all possible speed, that is to say, was doing just what every Russian desired. So what was the use of performing various operations on the French who were running away as fast as they possibly could?

Secondly, it would have been senseless to block the passage of men whose whole energy was directed to flight.

Thirdly, it would have been senseless to sacrifice one's own troops in order to destroy the French army, which without external interference was destroying itself at such a rate that, though its path was not blocked, it could not carry across the frontier more than it actually did in December, namely a hundredth part of the original army.

Fourthly, it would have been senseless to wish to take captive the Emperor, kings, and dukes—whose capture would have been in the highest degree embarrassing for the Russians, as the most adroit diplomatists of the time (Joseph de Maistre and others) recognized. Still more senseless would have been the wish to capture army corps of the French, when our own army had melted away to half before reaching Krásnoe and a whole division would have been needed to convoy the corps of prisoners, and when our men were not always getting full rations and the prisoners already taken were perishing of hunger.

All the profound plans about cutting off and capturing Napoleon and his army were like the plan of a market gardener who, when driving out of his garden a cow that had trampled down the beds he had planted, should run to the gate and hit the cow on the head. The only thing to be said in excuse of that gardener would be that he was very angry. But not even that could be said for those who drew up this project, for it was not they who had suffered from the trampled beds.

But besides the fact that cutting off Napoleon with his army would have been senseless, it was impossible.

It was impossible first because—as experience shows that a three-mile movement of columns on a battlefield never coincides with the plans—the probability of Chichagóv, Kutúzov, and Wittgenstein effecting a junction on time at an appointed place was so remote as to be tantamount to impossibility, as in fact thought Kutúzov, who when he received the plan remarked that diversions planned over great distances do not yield the desired results.

Secondly it was impossible, because to paralyze the momentum with which Napoleon's army was retiring, incomparably greater forces than the Russians possessed would have been required.

Thirdly it was impossible, because the military term "to cut off" has no meaning. One can cut off a slice of bread, but not an army.

To cut off an army—to bar its road—is quite impossible, for there is always plenty of room to avoid capture and there is the night when nothing can be seen, as the military scientists might convince themselves by the example of Krásnoe and of the Berëzina. It is only possible to capture prisoners if they agree to be captured, just as it is only possible to catch a swallow if it settles on one's hand. Men can only be taken prisoners if they surrender according to the rules of strategy and tactics, as the Germans did. But the French troops quite rightly did not consider that this suited them, since death by hunger and cold awaited them in flight or captivity alike.

Fourthly and chiefly it was impossible, because never since the world began has a war been fought under such conditions as those that obtained in 1812, and the Russian army in its pursuit of the French strained its strength to the utmost and could not have done more without destroying itself.

During the movement of the Russian army from Tarútino to Krásnoe it lost fifty thousand sick or stragglers, that is a number equal to the population of a large provincial town. Half the men fell out of the army without a battle.

And it is of this period of the campaign—when the army lacked boots and sheepskin coats, was short of provisions and without vodka, and was camping out at night for months in the snow with fifteen degrees of frost, when there were only seven or eight hours of daylight and the rest was night in which the influence of discipline cannot be maintained, when men were taken into that region of death where discipline fails, not for a few hours only as in a battle, but for months, where they were every moment fighting death from hunger and cold, when half the army perished in a single month—it is of this period of the campaign that the historians tell us how Milorádovich should have made a flank march to such and such a place, Tormásov to another place, and Chichagóv should have crossed (more than knee-deep in snow) to somewhere else, and how so-and-so "routed" and "cut off" the French and so on and so on.

The Russians, half of whom died, did all that could and should have been done to attain an end worthy of the nation, and they are not to blame because other Russians, sitting in warm rooms, proposed that they should do what was impossible.

All that strange contradiction now difficult to understand between the facts and the historical accounts only arises because the historians dealing with the matter have written the history of the beautiful words and sentiments of various generals, and not the history of the events.

To them the words of Milorádovich seem very interesting, and so do their surmises and the rewards this or that general received; but the question of those fifty thousand men who were left in hospitals and in graves does not even interest them, for it does not come within the range of their investigation.

Yet one need only discard the study of the reports and general plans and consider the movement of those hundreds of thousands of men who took a direct part in the events, and all the questions that seemed insoluble easily and simply receive an immediate and certain solution.

The aim of cutting off Napoleon and his army never existed except in the imaginations of a dozen people. It could not exist because it was senseless and unattainable.

The people had a single aim: to free their land from invasion. That aim was attained in the first place of itself, as the French ran away, and so it was only necessary not to stop their flight. Secondly it was attained by the guerrilla warfare which was destroying the French, and thirdly by the fact that a large Russian army was following the French, ready to use its strength in case their movement stopped.

The Russian army had to act like a whip to a running animal. And the experienced driver knew it was better to hold the whip raised as a menace than to strike the running animal on the head.